雲的

Story of Clouds

故事

About Story of Clouds

Clouds think and speak, as someone said. I cannot agree more, and I have no idea how I started loving clouds and their words.

"Story of Clouds" is actually an account of how I feel and think about the beauty of Nature, Love, and Life.

God has arranged many people around me in my road of growth, and some of them did touch my heart and bring me smiles and tears. I would like to thank them for enriching my life and enlightening me in the "Story of Clouds".

Whilst all the 100 photos in this book were my own original pictures, the "Rainbow" on the cover was actually taken by my mother, who, by sending me this picture, wished that I could learn to be positive, despite obstacles.

"Story of Clouds" is dedicated to my dear mother, who is now with Jesus.

"I am fine here, Mom." This is the ultimate message of the book.

雲的故事

曾經有人說過，雲是有感情的，雲會說話的。不知道從何時開始愛上雲，也愛上聽雲說話。

《雲的故事》希望讓大家欣賞到大自然的美，也訴說夢魂縈繞的情，以及對人生的感悟。

很感謝在我生命中出現過，令我哭過、笑過、感動過、心動過的人。你們豐富了我的人生，也豐富了《雲的故事》。

書內有一百幅照片，都是我親手拍攝的，唯獨封面的雨後彩虹，是我媽媽幾年前拍給我的，相信她希望我能從彩虹中領悟人生，樂觀地面對生活。

出版《雲的故事》……是希望此刻在天上的她知道，女兒活得安好……

About the Author

Wendy Chan is passionate but naive in photography and writing.

She loves photography because it trains her to look for the beauty of everything.

She enjoys writing because the magical power of language allows for different interesting interpretations.

However, as her skills are limited, the photos she took may often fail to reveal the authentic beauty, and the words she used may sometimes fail to fully express her emotions and thoughts.

After all, the limited interests, or the interesting limitations, are somehow the manifestation of her life... and even yours.

關於作者

　　雲滴‧塵 Wendy Chan，不懂攝影，但喜歡攝影，不擅寫作，但喜歡寫作。

　　喜歡攝影，是因為攝影時總會嘗試捕捉景物美麗的角度，不知不覺可以養成一種習慣，看所有事物，都選擇看美好的一面。

　　喜歡寫作，是因為覺得語言文字很有力量，能令人共鳴，又可讓不同人各自去領會、詮釋，非常有趣。

　　當然，攝影技術有限，往往未能把肉眼所見的美景準確捕捉到。有時也因詞窮，無法表達到某些情感、思緒。

　　也許，在「有趣」與「有限」之間徘徊，是雲滴‧塵的人生……也是大家的人生。

大帽山雲海日落......
充滿震撼和感恩的經歷......
愛上雲，愛上雲的故事......

The sunset amid the sea of clouds at
Tai Mo Shan....
an overwhelming experience filled with
gratitude and love....
for the clouds and their stories....

雲 的 故 事 ，
始 於 文 字 ，
始 於 語 言……
這 裡 是 我 的 根 ，
也 是 「 雲 的 故 事 」
的 根……

The origin
of my knowledge,
the origin of
"Story of Clouds"....

幸運遇上令人驚嘆的晚霞雲彩......
震撼心弦，着實是筆墨難以形容......

It was the stunning sunset glow that
explained what "beyond speech" really means.

齊賞雲海......

享受，就是分享和感受......

在大自然的壯觀盛景前，無分你我......

Let's share the joy whilst acclaiming
the masterpiece of mighty Nature....

人生的機會，
要好好把握，
因為，
路並不一定
長有......

Seize the day,
seize the chance....
The road may disappear
when the tide comes....

這幅相是我三年前在觀塘海濱影的。
我很喜歡。
它令我想起「救贖」：
耶穌光、救生圈，
以及躲避在凳下的小鴿子......
究竟「救贖」是倚靠主？援助？
還是自救？......

I took this picture in three years ago.
It reminds me of Salvation :
Light of Jesus, lifebuoy, and the little pigeon
protected itself under the seat.
Where are we going to find Salvation?

難忘一刻……
從山頂失望而回到山腰的剎那，
你在天空繪了這一幅油彩

An unforgettable moment,
a stunning masterpiece
you painted for me,
overshadowing my
disappointment
from the day....

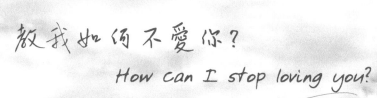

教我如何不愛你？

How can I stop loving you?

就是看到兩顆心……
並無改圖

I found two hearts by imagination,
not by Photoshop

永無止盡的溫柔......
Endless tender....

不信日落亦可這樣美……雲相信。

Clouds are charmed by the sunset,
the unbelievable beauty of the sunset.

天上雲，水中蓮，
都是抓不住的，
只能遠遠欣賞……
就像……

I can only admire
you at a distance....

緣份的天空……

你是哪一片？我又是哪一片？
我們會相遇嗎？

If our hearts are in the sky,
is there a place for me in yours?
Is there a place for you in mine?

把煩惱交給雲吧！

Let the clouds take your burden

不經意抬頭，
你竟給我驚喜

Your charm comes
with a surprise.

城門河……
有你的腳蹤，也有我的足跡，
可我們就是沒有相遇過……

We both walk along this adorable river,
in different times...
always....

我願做一片自在的雲
Let me float as the cloud...

是你太高？
還是我太低？
為什麼我們會相遇？

We met not by chance,
but by our efforts to break through
the paradigm....

此刻的你在掛念誰?

Who is in your mind at this moment?
Not me, I know.

再問一次，
究竟是你太高還是我太低？
我們又相遇了......今次在晚上......

We met again, day and night....
Is it a dream or what?

是光，穿透了雲的心，
也為雲帶來了色彩……

Light invaded the heart of clouds,
and coloured the clouds....
This is literally enlightenment.

風景源於心境。

美麗的回憶，醉人的風景。

It was impressive...

the scenery, and the memory.

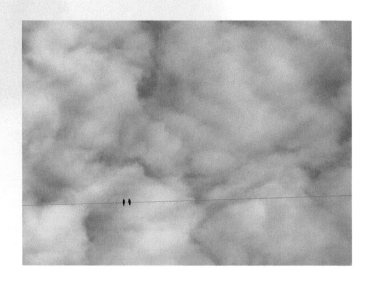

我們何時才可像牠倆，
一起欣賞藍天白雲啊？

Look forward to the moment...
when we sit side by side like them,
and the lovely clouds are above us....

雲在，情在。我心屬您……

Only clouds know my love to you

沒有雲，光不會這麼美，
沒有你，我找不到自己……

Let the light
excel amidst the clouds,
as I rekindle myself from you....

你是那麼漫不經意，
卻令人怦然心動……

My heart shivers with your breath....

有一刻,我很羨慕芒草,
可以輕撫白雲......

At that moment,
I wished I were the silver grass,
touching the clouds....

在美麗的天空下，
我們相遇了……
然後發現，
你有你的，
我有我的，
方向……

We met, and we left,
in different directions...
but the sky and
the clouds
are still there....

有一刻，我願化作鳥兒，
飛向白雲的懷抱……

At that moment,
I wished I were a bird,
heading to the clouds....

雲與小船，看似咫尺，
卻是永遠無法觸及之遙……
惟願大家向同一方飄浮，
方可繼續對望……

We are so close, and yet so far apart....
I can only follow your way, so that I can,
at least, keep you at my sight....

你是陰是晴？ 我該笑該哭？

Ups and downs, all for you

水中賞雲……
雲，其實也是水……你中有我，
我中有你……

When water mingles with clouds...
Wait, clouds are actually water...
just like you and me....

黃昏刹那，不但綿綿若絮，

還透出層層橙紅......

雲，就是有無限可能......

A magic moment with sunset glow

reflected through the candy floss....

Clouds, you are really magical!

原來，雲用自己本身的形態，

已經可以發光了。

Actually clouds can glow by

their own shape.

有沒有人看到，
遠處兩隻小白熊在談笑？

Am I the only one
who can see the two
white teddy bears?

多謝雲，
讓我欣賞到太陽的尾巴……
Thank you for the sunset,
my dear clouds...

雲是我的朋友......
他們有不同的外型、性格、特質，
也在我生活中擔當不同的角色

Clouds are my friends.
Different friends have different features,
playing different roles in my life....

心情好的時候，
雲是會起舞的。
今次應該是跳絲帶舞吧！

Let's enjoy the ribbon dance of the clouds!

雲有調皮的時候......

Naughty cloud...

雲也有發怒的時候......

When clouds get angry...

雲也會說不。

When the cloud says No

天空的美，
是屬於所有人的。
不論你身處何地，
只須輕輕抬頭，驚艷，
就在眼前……

The stunning sky
belongs to all of us.
Wherever, whenever,
whatever...
lift your head....

巧遇遠方雨雲，
灑下非常局部的雨……

It was a chance encounter...
a rain cloud with isolate shower....

你愛藍天，還是白雲？

每樣一半好嗎？

Let white and blue share the sky...

一個特別的清晨，一個特別的日子，
我想起特別的你......看不見太陽，
卻有光，有雲，有你......

A special dawn without the Sun,
a special day without you...
Oh, no... you are here,
with the light and clouds....

你不是在求偶，
為什麼要開屏呢？

Why are you flaunting
if you are not courting?

不是閃電，是雲……
卻觸及我內心深處……

Clouds, how come you flash into
my heart without flashing?

雲啊？
你怎麼總是圍着太陽呢？
你很喜歡光嗎？
放下，
你才可以成為一片自在的
雲……

Let go of your
admiration to the Sun,
Let go of your
adherence to the light,
Seize your own freedom....

水晶球裡看不到未來，
只看到，此刻的你，很美……

I don't bother about the future.
I just wish to look at you,
now and only now....

雲與青風，
可以常擁有⋯⋯

Seize the clouds
Seize the breeze
Seize the day

雲說，我會為你開一扇窗，
窗外更光亮。

The window of clouds is opened,
for all cloud lovers.

雲的角色……
不是要搶去夕陽的艷麗，
而是把夕陽的色彩立體地，
持續地，展現出來。

Clouds are the vivid manifestation
of sunset glow.
They are not thieves.

你喜歡藍天白雲的心經簡林，
還是迷霧瀰漫的心經簡林？
其實，
不論藍天白雲，
還是迷霧瀰漫，
心經簡林仍然是心經簡林。
Whether sunny or foggy,
woods are woods.
Only our perspective and
attitude change.

雲的深度，在於它的層次，
也在於它的變化萬千。

Clouds inspire me with
their sophistication and
dynamic manifestation.

孤獨......
solitude...

有時，厚厚的灰雲也很好……
沒有它，就看不到這種光芒了……

Gloomy clouds exist for the glow....

一個人看海的日子，
總有雲相伴。

The clouds are always
my companions, wherever,
whenever, however....

飄渺的綿雲下，是繁鬧的都市

雲，陪伴都市人
每天的營營役役……

The hustle and bustle of our city
is accompanied by the lovely clouds

雲化身為絲絲紅霞，
是最令人迷醉的時刻……
When clouds become rosy champagne,
I can never resist. Let me get drunk.

雲兒伴著太陽，
令天空熱鬧起來了！
The clouds are having
a party with the sun!

鱗鱗棉絮，皚皚雪道，
還有調皮的小球
在雪道滾動哩！

Clouds have made a piste for skiing
for their friend, with the audience
cheering in the mackerel sky....

富貴於我如浮雲……
但，浮雲於我又如珍寶……

Are you going to cloud your treasure
or treasure the cloud?

飛上天空，擁抱著綿綿的雲，
狠狠咬一口......
想必是很多孩子童年的夢想。

Fly up the sky, hug the clouds,
and have a big bite....
Wasn't it your dream
when you were a kid?

飄如絲，旋如風......
輕柔中有力度，
隨意，卻有方向......
這是雲曼妙之處......

Light but determined,
gentle yet passionate....
This is the personality of clouds,
the charm of clouds....

鏡子裡，
雲的世界是另一個色調......
會否帶來另一個故事？

Will a different tone from the mirror
reflect a different story?

凋零的楓、
灰沉的山、
散漫的雲……
聚合起來，
倒構作了一幅秋之交響曲。

A symphony of autumn comprises of
lonely red leaves, gloomy hills,
and casual clouds....

皚皚雪地上，只有寂寞的枯枝？
不！它們不寂寞，因為有雲……
只要上下倒轉來看，便明白了！
天與地，其實也是同氣連枝……

How is the sky different from the land?
It's a matter of orientation.
How is snow different from clouds?
It's a matter of perspective....

同一個維港，晴天雨天有不同的氣氛，
但亦各有特色，同樣吸引……
始終，變的是雲，是天氣，不是維港。
再想深一層，雲縱然是會變化，
變的也只是形態、顏色……
怎樣變，雲也始終是水滴……

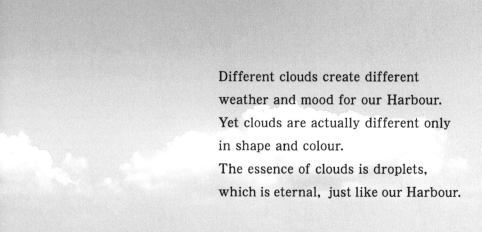

Different clouds create different
weather and mood for our Harbour.
Yet clouds are actually different only
in shape and colour.
The essence of clouds is droplets,
which is eternal, just like our Harbour.

多少年，雲兒陪伴著獅子，
也陪伴著這個都市……

Clouds are the companions of Lion,
and the city....

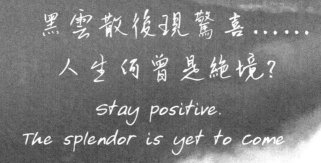

黑雲散後現驚喜......
人生何曾是絕境？
Stay positive.
The splendor is yet to Come

雲 上 的 燭 光　　Candle light on the cloud
{巴 士 隨 影}　　{Taken on the bus}

你這樣子出現，
究竟想表達些什麼呢？
What on earth do you
wish to express, my dear?

雲與山，分別在於，
山不能扮雲，但雲可以扮山。

How would you differentiate clouds and hills?
Well, clouds can become hills, but not vice versa....

雲中月，彷如貝裡藏珠⋯⋯
大自然，本身就是一個寶藏，
有待我們去發掘、欣賞⋯⋯

See the pearl amid the clouds?
Let's explore more treasure from Nature!

雲與夕陽一起照鏡子，
誰比誰美呢？

Who has more charm,
the cloud or the sunset?
Ask the mirror....

有些煩惱，
是沒有可能逃避，
沒有可能放下的。

只要接受了這個事實，
然後把煩惱緊緊擁抱著，
接受它成為自己或生命的一部分，
便會感覺它反而輕了......

Sometimes worries and agonies are inevitable.
Embrace them.
Accept that they are episodes of life.
Regard them as elements of yourself.
Maybe you will not feel their existence any more....

愛情是雲，醉人心弦，
卻飄忽不定，無法抓住。
友情是月，忠誠伴你……
不是天天看到它，
它卻永遠存在。

If love is an erratic cloud,
I would rather
have you as my friend,
like the moon,
that always stands by me...
whether I can see you or not.

風把雲帶來，
也把雲帶走……
誰也沒有欠誰，
只因這就是緣……

The wind brings the cloud,
not for anyone.

The wind takes the cloud,
not for any reason.

They come and they go,
as they are wind and cloud....

只有待雲飄走了，
才發現，
一直照亮我的，
是月……

The clouds disappeared,
and I eventually
realized that
the light was from
the moon

常說，一念天堂，一念地獄
關鍵也許不是選擇正確與否，
而是錯了能否回頭。

Sometimes, the crucial
point is not the choice,
but is the chance to
rechoose....

有時，雲也令光更添魅力……
雲與光，根本就是好朋友

Clouds and light are good partners.
They enhance each other.

雲啊！也許你變幻莫測，也許你很有情緒脾性……
我，就是喜歡你飄忽的美，喜歡你這麼有性格。
縱使天空的強光會刺痛我的眼睛，
我也不願把視線移開……
假若要我下一秒失明，
我也要在這一秒再看你一眼……

You haunt me with your dynamic float.
You blind me with your erratic charm.
I love you at my first sight... till my last sight.

黑雲底下的一線藍天，
提醒我們，凡事無絕對，
希望總存在......

The blue sky amid the dark clouds
reminds us that hope always exists,
though sometimes we need some patience

綿綿如雪也好，絲滑若冰也好，
雲在天際，該是冷的。可是，
在我心窩，雲永遠是那麼溫暖......

Clouds at high altitude
are icy and snowy,
but they touch my heart
with warmth and passion....

你知道她是誰嗎？

你知道她在等誰嗎？

雲知道。

Clouds know whom
she is waiting for.
Clouds are waiting
with her.

雲是夕陽的歸宿，
也是飛鳥的歸宿……
Clouds give shelter for
everyone, everything, everywhere....

是誰劃破你的嬌柔，
卻令你更添性格，更有韻味？

When the glow in the morning is
no longer intact, it becomes
more unique, and more charming....

天上看雲，另一種景緻......
不知道天外又有多少重天呢？

We may wish to enjoy the
clouds high above in the sky....
But where is the highest?
Is there a highest?

晴天雨天，各有佳境……
這不是自我安慰……
而且，我相信，即使烏雲密佈，
也不是世界末日。

Learn to enjoy the beauty of
gloomy clouds.... After all,
no matter dark cloud or bright cloud,
neither one can dominate forever....

雲為禿枝添上生命活力，
也在困境中，
為大家帶來希望。

Clouds bring leaves
to the bare branches.
Hopes never end.

雲，見證了幾許偶遇、
相逢、別離、緣起緣滅……
People say hi, say bye all under the sky.

憑著我們的信仰，
憑著我們的信念，
人生總是充滿希望……

Our hope comes from our belief....

這幅相是兩年前在尖沙咀拍的，
當時原本想期待鹹蛋黃日落……

一直記着這首詩歌的詞：

"神未曾應許，天色常藍……
常樂無痛苦，常安無虞……
神卻曾應許，生活有力……
無限的體諒，不死的愛！"

This picture was taken two years ago at
Tsim Sha Tsui.
I remember the disappointment when
the sunset was not as expected.

Yet I also remember this song :

" God hath not promised skies always blue...
Joy without sorrow, peace without pain...
But God hath promised...
strength for the day...
Unfailing sympathy, undying love. "

雲的盡處究竟在哪裡呢？

Where is the end of clouds?

雲的盡處，是無盡的恩典……

The end of clouds, is the endless grace

曾經天天相對，
失去才懂得不捨……
可是，不捨，也得放手……
人生就是如此。

Treasure before it's gone.
Let go after it's gone.

留下，只有，思念

I miss you. Mom.

後記

I suddenly realise that apart from the cover photo, the very last picture of this book was also not taken by me...but by my daughter.

Story of Clouds is perhaps also a story of...inheritance.

　　寫到最後，才發現，原來除了封面的雨後彩虹之外，書末那幅照片，也不是我拍的。

　　拍照的人，是我的女兒。

　　雲的故事，原來也是一個傳承的故事……

雲的故事

Story of Clouds

作者：雲滴·塵
編輯：青森文化編輯組
設計：VN Chan

出版：紅出版（青森文化）
地址：香港灣仔道133號卓凌中心11樓
出版計劃查詢電話：(852) 2540 7517
電郵：editor@red-publish.com
網址：http://www.red-publish.com

香港總經銷：聯合新零售(香港)有限公司
台灣總經銷：貿騰發賣股份有限公司
新北市中和區立德街136號6樓
(886) 2-8227-5988
http://www.namode.com

出版日期：2022年5月
圖書分類：攝影/流行讀物
ISBN：978-988-8743-97-1
定價：港幣80元正/新台幣320元正